THE ICE MAN

by

ROGER HURN AND JANE A.C. WEST

Illustrated by Stik

Tribe
Book 3

To the real Finn – for being so cool.

With special thanks to:

Wa'fy Abdullah
Kai Bennett
Emma Crane
Annabel Dannheim
Elizabeth Duffy
Luc Issolah
Annalee Mullins
Max Murphy
Emily North
Rishil Patel
Harry Rainton
William Rose
Oliver Stuart
Kyle Tagg
Lorraine Tilly

First published in 2011 in Great Britain by
Barrington Stoke Ltd
18 Walker St, Edinburgh, EH3 7LP

www.barringtonstoke.co.uk

ISBN: 978-1-84299-601-0

Printed in China by Leo

The publisher gratefully acknowledges support from the Scottish Arts
Council towards the publication of this title.

Scottish
Arts Council

WHO ARE TRIBE?

ARE THEY HUMANS?

OR ARE THEY ANIMALS?

Tribe are humans *and* animals.

They are super-heroes with special powers.

They can *shape-shift* – change from animals to humans and back again.

THEIR PLAN: to save the world from anyone who tries to destroy it.

Tribe need to find the bad guys – before it's too late.

The Earth is in trouble – and only Tribe have the power to help.

Tribe are helped by TOK – the Tree Of Knowledge.

Tribe can travel all over the world using the roots of trees.

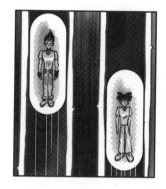

Tribe also have the power to talk to animals – and they can send each other mind-messages, even when they are miles apart.

CAST LIST

Finn

Bruin

Kat

Mo

Talon

Vana

and ...

Ty Koone

Contents

Chapter 1
Chilling Out

Tribe were in their Head Quarters in a huge oak tree, the Tree Of Knowledge (TOK). Talon was playing chess with Vana. Bruin and Mo were watching *Dr Who* and Finn was looking at the Sap Screen.

"What are you doing, Finn?" growled
Vana.

"Looking for trouble," said Finn.

"There's no need to look for trouble,
Finn," said Vana. "Trouble will find you."

"Yes," agreed Bruin. "Trouble is Finn's
middle name."

"No, it isn't," said Kat. "It's Fishy."

Finn wasn't listening. He was gazing
hard at the screen. "Look at this," he said.

The others got up and stood round the screen. It showed a picture of the Arctic wilderness taken from space. A red light flashed on a place called Caribou Bay.

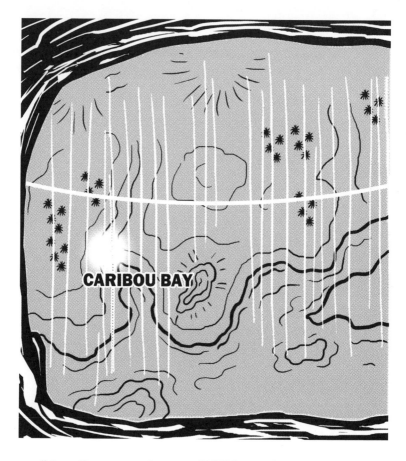

"Caribou Bay's a wildlife refuge area where hunting is banned," said Vana.

"So why is the red light flashing?" said Finn.

"Let's ask TOK," said Talon. TOK was the voice of the tree-house.

Vana was in charge as always. "OK, TOK, what's going on?"

TOK began to speak. "The people there say that an evil demon called the Ice Man has come back to Caribou Bay. He brings death and destruction. You must stop him."

Tribe felt a shiver of fear run down their spines.

"Get your winter woollies, guys," roared Bruin. "We're going to find the Ice Man – and that's *snow* joke!"

Chapter 2
The Warning

Tribe came racing into Caribou Bay on ski-doos. They jumped off their machines and looked around. The bay was deserted.

Vana sniffed the air. "I can smell fear," she said.

"No, that's Finn's feet you can smell," said Kat. "He's wearing six pairs of dirty socks!"

"The dirt keeps the cold out," said Finn. "And, boy, is it cold! What do people eat for lunch round here – *ice-burgers* with *chilli* sauce?"

"No, we hunt caribou for our food, just like we've always done," said a voice from behind them. "Who are you and what are you doing here?"

Standing behind them was a small man dressed in clothes made from caribou skins.

Tribe were amazed that they had not heard

him creep up on them.

Vana growled. The hood of the man's jacket was trimmed with wolf fur!

Talon stepped up to the man and spoke to him. He knew this was not the time to get angry. "We are Tribe and we're here to find out what is happening with the Ice Man."

"Yes," said Mo. "We want to help you and your people."

The man gave a short, bitter laugh. "Go back to your own lands while you still can. You cannot help us. My people have fled.

No one can beat the Ice Man. If you try, he will kill you."

He turned and walked away.

Chapter 3
Ice Dream

"Wow, that man will freeze us out if he can," said Finn.

"How come *he's* still here if all his people have gone?" asked Bruin

"I don't trust him," snarled Vana.

"Why did none of us hear him creeping up behind us?" said Mo.

"Yeah," said Kat. "Only mice like you, Mo, are as quiet as that."

"Follow him, Talon," said Bruin. "Keep your eagle eye on him."

Talon morphed into a huge eagle. He beat his wings and soared up into the sky.

He soon spotted the little man. He was driving along the forest trail on a sled pulled by a team of huskies. The poor dogs were running as fast as they could but the man was using a whip to try to make them run even faster. This made Talon very angry.

He was just about to swoop down and snatch the whip from the man's hand when he saw something terrible. The forest trail ended at a wide clearing in the forest. And there, right in the middle of the clearing, was an oil rig!

19

The man jumped off the sled and hurried across to a large log cabin next to the rig. He pulled open the door and went inside.

Then Talon saw a wolf standing at the edge of the forest. It was Vana. She ran across the clearing and up to where the huskies lay panting on the ground. Talon flew down to join her.

The huskies lifted their heads and growled at Vana and Talon. They were too tired to do more than that.

"It's OK, " said Vana. "We're not here to fight. We just want to know what's going on."

"Bad things," said the husky leader. "Our master, Irniq, had a secret meeting here in the forest with a man called Ty Koone."

Vana's lips curled back into a snarl. "Ty Koone is an evil man, boss of a huge oil company. He will stop at nothing to get what he wants. He is breaking the law by drilling for oil in a wildlife reserve." Vana looked as if she wanted to rip Ty Koone to bits.

Talon put his wing across his sister's back. "Cool it, Vana," he said. "Our friend the husky has more to tell."

The dog nodded. "Ty Koone wanted to get rid of all the people who live round here so he could drill for oil in secret. He paid Irniq a lot of money to help him."

"What did Irniq do?" asked Vana.

"Irniq told Ty Koone the old story of the Ice Man. Then he told the people that he had seen the Ice Man in a dream. He said the Ice Man was going to destroy the village so everyone must leave at once."

"Did they?" asked Talon.

"No, they didn't want to go," said the husky leader. "But then, a few days later, the Ice Man came and chased the people away from the village."

"A demon Ice Man? No way," snapped

Vana. "Ty Koone faked it."

"Maybe," said the husky. "But when the people had gone, men came with Ty Koone and built the oil rig."

Vana was very angry now. "OK, Mr Ty Koone, the big bad wolf is coming to get you," she said.

But, before she could move, the Ice Man came out of the forest and stomped towards them!

Chapter 4
The Ice Man

"What is that thing?" screeched Talon.

A blast of icy blue air shot out of the Ice Man's mouth. Talon and Vana jumped out of the way just in time.

The Ice Man stomped across the clearing. It was tall, white and hairy. Its mouth had rows of huge fangs that looked like icicles.

"Look out, Vana!" yelled Talon. "If it bites us, we're going to get more than just frost bite!"

Another blast of icy blue air whizzed past their ears.

"That's not a demon. It's a robot and Ty Koone is in control of it," snarled Vana. "Look!"

Ty Koone, wearing his big cowboy hat, had stepped out of the cabin. He was holding a remote control pad to make the Ice Man move. Irniq, the man with the whip, was at his side.

"I'll fix him," shouted Talon. "You save the huskies."

Talon flew over the Ice Man's head while Vana bit through the straps that tied the huskies to the sled. The huskies shot off out of the Ice Man's way.

Vana tried to follow them but she slipped on the snow. She fell and twisted her paw. The Ice Man loomed over her. It opened its jaws and took aim. It couldn't miss!

Chapter 5
Melt Down

Ty Koone giggled. "Hey, Wolf," he yelled. "You've heard of hot dogs? Well, the Ice Man's going to turn you into a very *cold* dog!"

His finger was on the button. But before he could press it, Talon came screaming down from the sky and snatched the control pad from his hand.

"Give that back, you scruffy bunch of feathers!" yelled Ty Koone, red with fury.

"Don't worry, boss. I'll get it back for you," said Irniq.

The little man aimed his whip at Talon. But six huge huskies jumped on him and knocked the whip out of his hand. He vanished under a pile of very angry dogs.

Talon took careful aim and dropped the control pad. It was a direct hit! It bounced off Ty Koone's big hat and shattered in the snow. Ty Koone toppled over like a falling tree. Talon had knocked him out cold!

The Ice Man stopped. Sparks flew out of its ears, nose and mouth. It shook. Then the Ice Man burst into flames and began to melt.

It fell back into the oil rig. There was a big crunch. The Ice Man was stuck in the oil well! The oil well was blocked. Ty Koone yelled with rage. "My oil! How will I get my oil now?"

Talon flew over to Vana. "I see things got too hot for the Ice Man," he said.

Vana nodded. "Yes, it should have taken a chill pill."

Talon chuckled. "Ty Koone couldn't beat Tribe – his oil well plan isn't going so *well* now!"

DRILLING FOR OIL WILL KILL WILDLIFE IN THE ARCTIC!

The Arctic National Wildlife Refuge is a safe place for wildlife. Arctic foxes, caribou, birds, wolves, brown bears and polar bears all live there. But people want to drill for oil in this lovely place.

The oil companies say there is enough oil in the Refuge to fill 10 billion barrels. But drilling for oil could destroy the habitats of many wild animals and birds. Some kinds of animals, like polar bears, might be wiped out.

The oil from the Refuge will all be used up in just over a year, but the wilderness will be lost forever.

To find out more about the Artic National Wildlife Refuge go to: http://arctic.fws.gov/.

VANA – WOLF GIRL

BRAVE, THE LEADER OF THE PACK.

TALON'S TWIN SISTER.

SPECIAL SKILL: can smell trouble.

LOVES: running wild, full moons.

HATES: people who wear fur.

MOST LIKELY TO SAY: "Tonight is my night to howl."

BIGGEST SECRET: being a wolf sometimes frightens her.

TRIBE TALK!

To: Vana

From: Sally

Subject: Wildlife

Hi Vana,

How can I make my back garden wildlife friendly?

Sally

To:	Sally
From:	Vana
Subject:	Re: Wildlife

Hi Sally!

You can put up a nesting box. Then wild birds will come to your garden. But if you have a pet cat, put a bell round its neck. This will warn the birds when your pet is out to catch them!

Your growl pal,

Vana

FYI: WOLVES

 • Wolves do not eat people, no matter what fairy tales say!

 • A female wolf can weigh as much as 36kg. A male wolf can weigh as much as 50kg.

 • Wolves live in packs.

• Wolves can sprint at a speed of 61km per hour for short distances!

 • Wolves almost never attack humans.

 • Human beings are the biggest danger to wolves. We destroy their habitats and hunt them.

JOKE OF THE DAY

VANA: What happened when the wolf ate the clown?

BRUIN: I don't know...

VANA: He felt a bit funny!

CHECK OUT THE REST OF
THE TRIBE BOOKS!

For more info check out our website:
www.barringtonstoke.co.uk